THE MAZE

AN EXTREME HORROR STORY

JORDON GREENE

FRANKLIN/KERR
CONCORD, NORTH CAROLINA

Published by Franklin/Kerr Press, LLC
349-L Copperfield Boulevard #502 | Concord, North Carolina 28025
1.704.659.3915 | info@franklinkerr.com
www.FranklinKerr.com

For information about special discounts available for bulk purchases, sales
promotions, fund-raising and educational needs, contact Franklin/Kerr Press
Sales at 704-659-3915 or sales@franklinkerr.com.

Edited by Chelly Peeler
Cover & Interior design by Jordon Greene

Printed in the United States of America

FIRST EDITION

ISBN-10: 0-9983913-3-6
ISBN-13: 978-0-9983913-3-5

Fiction: Horror
Fiction: Thriller
Fiction: Splatterpunk

To Joseph Hartley
for being a constant friend and
the beginning of my literary journey.

ACKNOWLEDGMENTS

As this is my first foray into the world of extreme horror, AKA lot of blood and gore, it was great to have a number of people working with me to help fine tune and get the story ready for you. My editor, Chelly Peeler, was amazing as always. Every time she edits my work it's crazy how much I realize I still have to learn. Thanks to Dawn White as well, my proofreader, for being there to catch what the rest of us didn't.

A big thanks goes out to my beta readers, the ones who dig in and read the story after I finish my initial drafts, the ones who have to deal with all the stupid errors and issues. I was glad to have David Kummer, a fellow horror author, return to beta read this story. Thanks to my friends and beta readers Amanda Jane and Kevin & Chelsea Enloe for providing me some invaluable feedback on corrections and improvements.

Although his suggestions did end up adding about one-thousand words to an already long "short story" (some might claim it's a novella, but I'm sticking with short story), I have to give special thanks to Chris Hollar. Chris's suggestions led to some substantial changes that I hope and believe will provide a better and more satisfying read.

I also want to thank Billy and Andy at Pier 51 Seafood Restaurant in Concord, NC, my writing location of choice, for not kicking me out for staying too long. Thanks to Laura, Pam, Lynn, McKenzie and Deanna for dealing with me taking up a booth for hours at a time, you all have been so gracious and kind to me.

If you're ever in Concord, NC don't miss out on Pier 51, it's the best seafood (and salad bar) around.

1

The old Taurus bounced over another pothole, courtesy of the South Carolina Department of Transportation's lackluster repair schedule. To be fair, it wasn't exactly a major roadway like HWY-17 spanning the Myrtle Beach coastline, the road they had abandoned for this backwoods adventure.

Kayden Walker sat in the back seat, long slender legs half covered in khaki cargo shorts sprawled out on the empty space beside him, his back against the door. A set of black ear buds drowned out his parents in the front seat and their "classic" music with a steady stream of rumbling drum rolls and guitar riffs. He bobbed his head to the beat, mumbling the lyrics while he scrolled through the list of songs on his iPod. Finding his favorite Bad Omens tune, he tapped the screen and let his gaze drift up to the window and out at the passing countryside.

He watched the leaves fall while the heavy industrial beat built in his ears. Droves of brown, yellow, orange and every shade in between blanketed the roadside and spotted the thinning branches of the forest bordering the passing road. Kayden was thankful the heater was working today. It often chose to take the day off and his dad, a diesel mechanic by trade, hadn't yet had the time to figure out the problem.

It was day four of the family vacation, the same vacation that got Kayden out of school one whole week every October despite his teachers' protests. With cold setting in, less people came to the coast during the autumn months and the overall cost after Labor Day made it fit within his parents' budget better. Usually Kayden would have jumped on the opportunity to miss school, but this year was different. There was a girl back home, Mira Brooks, who Kayden was certain he couldn't be away from for more than a day. He'd spent the trip texting and Snapchatting her, and occasionally Mike, his friend since the fifth grade.

Usually Teagan, Kayden's older brother, would be in the seat next to Kayden teasing his younger sibling and doing what older brothers do when you're stuck in a car for hours on end. His college classes up in Boston had not been as forgiving this time, so the trip had become the first without Teagan that Kayden had ever been on.

A small white house streaked past the opposite window, piles of leaves heaped high in the small front lawn. A street sign Kayden didn't bother to read lapsed by and then more trees. They'd been on the road driving west out of Myrtle Beach for at least thirty minutes. Tammy, Kayden's mom, had found mention of a seasonal maze out in Conway that claimed to be a family-friendly event that went "all out" for Halloween. The outdated website didn't look to hold much promise. With so many attractions closed or not open until late during the off-season, the first item on their loosely arranged agenda had quickly become the maze.

Kayden tapped the screen on his phone, switching the music off, and opened the Snapchat app. His face appeared on the screen. The sheer number of pale brown freckles on his otherwise unblotted skin gave the appearance of a mild beige complexion where little truly existed. His honey eyes and broad chin stared back at him. He held down the circle at the bottom of the screen.

"This maze better have some cool shit, because it's taking forever to get there," he told the phone, letting his finger off the screen. He added the video to his Snapchat story as a hand tapped his thigh. Kayden reached up and pulled out his left earbud, meeting his mother's glaring eyes up front.

"Watch your language, Kayden," Tammy chided, rose-pink lips pursed and her golden-brown eyes, with a subtle hint of green bordering the irises, bearing down on him.

"Yes, ma'am," Kayden frowned. He was about to put the earbud back in place, but stopped. "How much longer 'til we get there?"

"GPS says another six minutes." It was his dad, Kenneth, Jr., or Ken as everyone really called him, his eyes glued to the road ahead of them. His voice boomed to the back seat. Ken wasn't a big man exactly. He was tall and slim, a Marine in a past life, but all that beer had finally begun to award him with the beginnings of the coveted beer belly.

"Agh!" Kayden groaned.

"Come on, it's not that far," Tammy reasoned, a light southern drawl peppering her words.

"Nothing takes this long to get to back home," Kayden argued.

"You've obviously never sat in morning traffic on seventy-seven yet," Ken took his eyes off the road long enough to give his wife a sideways grin. "You do realize we only live like eleven miles from my job and sometimes it takes me just under an hour to get home from work, right?"

"Yeah, I guess." Kayden shrugged. He'd never really given any thought to it. He returned his attention to his phone and sent out a text to Mira. *It's taking forever to get to this damn maze. It better be good!*

A few minutes later, a mid-sized warehouse appeared up ahead off the right shoulder just as the GPS announced, "You have arrived." It was an old structure. Rust had eaten away at the metal sheets where the angled roofline met the front facing wall. A makeshift double window, obviously installed later in the building's history, set next to a single-entry door. A handwritten sign to the right of the door announced the Halloween Maze would be open the whole month of October.

Ken pulled the car off the road as Kayden's phone vibrated in his hand and dinged. He felt the tires meet gravel and grind to a halt next to two other vehicles, an old Ram and a newer model Kia sedan. Kayden checked his phone, a new message from Mira.

It's gotta be better than sitting in Ms. T's History class.

"All right, here we are," Ken announced, as if his wife and son were totally blind to the fact. He looked over to Tammy, "I really hope this is more like a kiddy Halloween maze. I'm not too thrilled about having the sh—crap scared out of me."

Kayden rolled his eyes. It had been at his mom's insistence that the family skip a movie for the maze; she loved the eerie and scary. Kayden couldn't blame her. Now that he didn't suffer from horror movie-induced nightmares anymore, he thoroughly enjoyed it, too. He couldn't count the number of times he'd stayed up late with his mom watching scary movies that she forbade him from telling his dad she'd allowed him to watch. But he was worried it was going to be just as his dad hoped, some kiddy-sensitive maze missing all the bells and whistles of real fright.

"Oh, you'll be fine," Tammy assured him with a gentle hand on his shoulder and then stepped out of the car.

Kayden sent Mira a quick *I've got to go, love you* text and then pulled out the one remaining earbud still in his ear and threw the pair on the seat. He pocketed his phone and swung the door open, crunching his feet onto the gravel parking lot. Shutting the door behind him, he caught up with his dad and mom at the front of the old sedan. He eyed the new car sitting a few feet away, its gentle curves and subtle prowess a stark contrast to the rounded ends of his parents' vehicle.

"Come on, let's go," Tammy urged them, putting a hand on Ken's back and pushing him forward.

Kayden grinned. It wasn't often that his dad showed signs of fear.

Going stone-faced, Ken pushed through the front door. A bell rang, announcing their entrance and revealing a musty old room in shades of brown and grey. The floor was bare concrete, the walls covered in cheap wood paneling that peeled at the seams in places. A counter sat a few feet within, cold checkered laminate encasing the tabletop and more wood paneling bordering its edges. A tall behemoth of a man stood behind the counter.

He looked to be in his late twenties, standing at least six feet, maybe taller, sea green eyes staring blankly at Kayden then his parents as they walked in and shut the door. He had blond hair, cut short, almost buzzed, and a set of broad muscular shoulders hid under a shirt that was a bit too small for him. A trivial scowl that he didn't bother to mask marked his lips, like he wasn't happy they'd barged in to this attraction during his shift. He didn't say a word as Ken stepped up to the counter.

"Uh…hello," Ken started, awkwardly breaking the silence. He found the name badge on the man's chest. "Jasper. We're here for the Halloween maze."

"It's five dollars per person," Jasper blurted, his voice calm but dull. "You from out of town?"

"Yeah, Charlotte," Ken told him.

That seemed to please Jasper, a hint of a smile breaking his stoic demeanor.

"That's good. Makes the maze more interesting when it's all out-of-towners. No one to spoil the fun that way."

Kayden raised his brow at the man's curt manner as he swept his eyes around the small room. Knick-knacks were everywhere. Jack-o-lanterns, big fake spiders, ghosts and ghouls. He stopped on a young couple standing just a few feet behind him by the entry door. Kayden let the left edge of his lip curve up in a half grin. The two strangers smiled back.

The man was tall and lanky, his forest green eyes set behind rimless spectacles below short brown hair and prominent ears. The girl seemed to be from a different world. She was short, probably five-foot-two, with a slim shapely body, nice hips, a full round buttocks in short khaki shorts. Kayden loved it when a girl cut her hair like the beauty before him. It was cut to the skin on the left side of her head, but left long, straight and blue as it draped just above her right shoulder. An inconspicuous tattoo was stamped just above her collarbone, the Batman logo.

"Okay," Ken replied awkwardly, pulling out his wallet and passing over the admission fee to Jasper.

On the other side of the room, along the same counter that the unusual clerk stood behind, Kayden found a pile of tools. He wandered over while his dad was getting his change back and fingered through the items. A battery-powered nail gun, a knot of rope, thick nails, some tools Kayden didn't recognize and a large knife that looked a lot like the old Ka-Bar his dad said he used when he was in the Marines.

"Hey!" a thick voice boomed. It was the clerk behind the counter. "Don't touch those."

"Sorry," Kayden stepped back. "What's all this for?"

"They're my tools for the maze. I never know what I'm going to need in there," Jasper explained, reaching for the tools and placing them somewhere out of reach under the counter, eyeing Kayden suspiciously.

"Oh, you also do upkeep for the maze?" Tammy inquired.

"Yes, ma'am," Jasper coughed, covering his mouth, and then continued. "It's my baby. I maintain it all."

"That's nice." She nodded.

"Well, now that everyone's squared away, if you're ready, you can all start the maze. Goal's simple. Try to get out."

"Is there a time limit?" It was the pretty girl behind them. Kayden turned to look at her. She was attractive, but his girl Mira was even more of a looker. At the thought, he pulled out his phone and sent her another text.

Time for this stupid maze. Wish me luck.

"Oh, yeah. You get one hour. If you don't get out in an hour, you have to stay." Jasper put his hands up and wiggled his fingers, his voice raising a note but failing to deliver the eerie undertone.

The girl grinned and nodded, as did the others.

"And no phones," Jasper barked, staring at Kayden who grinned back innocently. "All phones and recording devices go in this lock box. Don't need no one spoiling the fun for others."

Jasper turned and inserted a key in a small grey box on a cabinet along the back wall and then put his hand out for everyone's phones. Once they were secured away, Jasper rounded the counter and stepped up to the only other door in the room. He grinned for the first time since the Walkers entered the building.

"I'll let you through this door, then you'll be in a small hallway which will lead to the maze entrance. Once you're in the hallway, I'll shut this door and it'll lock."

Kayden's dad looked at his mom and smirked. She was glowing. Kayden glanced at the couple out of the side of his vision and their smiles told him they were excited like his mom, besides the hint of reservation in the guy's face.

Jasper's grin vanished; he resumed his stoic personality as he opened the door, revealing a dimly lit hall.

"Have fun, and see ya in hell."

Kayden and the others moved past Jasper and into the room. Ken's mouth gaped open slightly and he leaned closer to Tammy.

"Is that really appropriate?" Ken commented more than asked.

Tammy waved him off and moved down the hallway. Kayden followed, keeping close to his parents. He wasn't a coward by a long shot, but the best way to get through a maze wasn't splitting up, at least according to his brain's logic. His eyes surveyed the room. The walls were built out of simple planks from floor to ceiling and more concrete floors with two standard, flickering, florescent bulbs dangling above.

"Hey," the pretty girl said, stepping up beside the Walkers. "I'm Florence, and this is my husband, Oscar."

"Good to meet you," Ken said, shaking Oscar's hand. "I'm sorry. I feel so rude; we didn't introduce ourselves out there. I'm Ken, this is my wife, Tammy, and my youngest son, Kayden."

"It's okay," Oscar assured him. He cocked an eyebrow and nodded toward the door that had just been closed behind them. "That clerk out there's really something. Sort of creepy."

"Yeah, really," Ken agreed.

"All part of the theatrics for the maze," Tammy said. "He's just trying to spook us before we get in there."

"Exactly," Florence agreed, nudging Oscar.

"I guess you two are on vacation, too?" Tammy asked.

"Yeah, well, honeymoon actually." Oscar beamed.

"Oh! Congrats!" Tammy almost yelled. Kayden rolled his eyes in the dark. Girls always get so excited at the thought of marriage. "That's awesome!"

"Congrats," Ken echoed his wife.

"Thanks," the couple said, almost in unison.

"Can we get started?" Kayden chimed in, pointing toward the door at the end of the hallway. "We've only got an hour to get out of here."

"Good point," Oscar agreed, shaking his head with an understanding grin. "Let's get going. I guess we should split up to cover more ground, so we'll see you at the end."

"Sounds good," Tammy nodded before Ken could speak up. They closed the remaining yards to the next door and Ken grasped the knob and opened it.

A rush of warm, stale air enveloped them, and a rancid rotting stench bit Kayden's nostrils.

"Oh fuck," Oscar blurted, earning himself an elbow in the side from Florence and a wide-eyed expression. He squinted and shrugged, realizing his mistake, but kept his mouth shut.

Kayden covered his nose and grinned at his parents' expressions, something between disgust and irritation. He wasn't sure at which they were disgusted more.

The smell was horrid. It reminded him of the sickening smell inside the walls of the Hollywood Wax Museum's Zombie Outbreak, a type of haunted house but with zombie's instead of ghosts. His nostrils flared at the odor, the stench of rotting flesh mixed with the stale odor of an old warehouse.

"Oh, that's horrid," Tammy complained, waving a hand in front of her face while her other hand covered her nose.

Keeping one hand over his nose, Kayden placed a palm on his mom's back and urged her forward, into the maze. They stepped in. It was dark, mustier than the entrance had been, and filled with noises. Red and orange lights splashed across the bare beamed ceiling and over the tall ten-foot walls built of an assortment of woods, fake greenery and other materials. Eerie music infiltrated the space, a mix of gloomy tones and quiet cackles interrupted by violent simulated screams.

Six feet ahead was the first choice. A fork with three different options, only one presumably leading to the exit, or maybe any of them would. Kayden eyed the left most opening, then the middle and the last. They all looked the same.

"We'll take the middle," Florence whispered, like someone else might hear them over the moans and screams playing overhead. She pointed toward the central path.

"Yeah, and we'll take the one on the left," Tammy said, craning her neck around to look at Kayden, brow raised as if in question.

"Sure," Kayden shrugged. "Why not?"

"We'll see you at the end, or sooner," Florence waved as she took Oscar by the arm and drug him off. The boy waved curtly and let himself be pulled along, disappearing around a turn a few yards away. Kayden could see that the maze must have been Florence's idea, not Oscar's, much like it had been his mom's idea, not his dad's.

"Here we go, guys." Tammy grinned and started walking forward.

Ken huffed and followed along with Kayden a step ahead, quickly overtaking his mother and shooting into the far-left opening. The path was only about six feet across, bordered by the same massive wooden walls that constructed the first room. A low moan echoed over the barrier from somewhere else in the maze, or maybe it was just over the speakers. Vines overtook a section of the maze ahead. Kayden stopped and reached out to touch the leaves; plastic.

Moving on, they veered off at the next left and Tammy immediately jumped back. A large replica of a rat sat in the corner, its eyes glowering.

"We come to a Halloween maze, and a fake rat's what scares you?" Ken laughs.

"Yeah!" Tammy defended herself, slapping Ken on the shoulder. "It's a *big* fake rat."

She skirted around the vermin, keeping a safe distance. Kayden shook his head and jogged past her, keeping an eye out for the next turn now that his vision had acclimated to the rotating and shifting glow of the red, white and orange lighting. He let his hand leave his nose, bearing the acrid smell. Beyond the occasional vine and the lights, the maze was simple and cold. It felt like Jasper didn't realize it was autumn outside and had opted to keep the air conditioner running, or at the very least failed to turn on the heater this morning. Kayden set off around the next corner, taking a right, checking behind him just long enough to be sure his mom and dad were following along.

It was more of the same. He tried to raise himself on his toes to get a better view of their location within the maze with respect to the perimeter of the building. It was a waste of time and energy. The privacy fence-like maze walls served as true blockades to any extra information, too high to get a real grasp on the size of the building or your location relative to any of its four edges.

A shrill scream broke through the music, sending a shiver up Kayden's spine. He stopped for a brief second before realizing it was just the music. He mentally cursed himself and set his feet back into motion. At sixteen, the last thing he wanted his mom to do was ask if he was okay.

Without explanation the lights flickered, then failed entirely, drowning Kayden in a sea of absolute black. Behind him, something shuffled in the darkness. Kayden spun around, the hair on his neck tingling and on end.

"Mom? Dad?" Kayden called out blindly, his eyes flicking from corner-to-corner, hoping to catch some shadow in the void. "You there?"

"We're here, Kayden," Ken's voice reached back to him, only a foot or two away at most.

Kayden let his body continue to turn, already losing his sense of direction in the dark. Suddenly, the lights blasted back on and Kayden squinted under the sudden burst of light. His mother's scream pierced his ears just as his eyes set on the wicked face staring back at him, only inches from his nose.

"What the *hell*?" Kayden screamed, faltering back a step as the lights dropped again and suddenly blinked back to life.

Kayden shot his eyes around the empty space. It was gone. Those charged green orbs, not eyes, that face, gone. In the instant before the lights flickered off again, Kayden had taken in the rough grisly skin. It was an amalgam of burnt orange, crimson and black, lines running up and down a circular head. Huge jack-o-lantern voids filled with electrical green currents where eyes should have been. Rotted black, serrated teeth stretched abnormally far across the lower half of the face along the upper and bottom jaw and a dirty bandage wrapped its way over a bloodied scalp. The person, whoever it was, had a grisly looking pumpkin over their face.

"Where'd it go?" Kayden yelled, staring back at his parents.

"I don't know," Ken shot back, eyes flicking back and forth, searching the corridor for any signs of the jack-o-lantern-masked figure. "Let's just keep going so we can get out of here."

"That was incredible!" Kayden's mom chimed in, holding a hand over her heaving chest. "Horrifying, but crazy. Sure didn't take long either."

"Yeah, that *was* awesome," Kayden agreed with a huge grin, trying to hide the fear that had gripped him as the unexpected face had peered into his eyes. He let himself take a few deep breaths to regulate his pulse, shaking his head. "Definitely not a kiddy maze."

2

Another scream pierced through the dark just before the lights came back on. Florence clenched tightly to Oscar's hand, her body pressed against his.

"Damn, this place is creepy," Oscar whispered. "I thought it was supposed to be some stupid backwoods maze, not a let's-scare-you-out-of-your-damn-mind maze."

"Oh, calm down, Oscar," Florence chided him, loosening her grip on his palm and letting herself move to his side again. She wouldn't admit that she was spooked. It was all fake, but it still scared her, but that was the point. Why else voluntarily walk into a place like this? "It was just the lights."

"Yeah, just the lights. Who cuts off the lights on a bunch of tourists in a dark maze?" Oscar already missed the feeling of her body against his the moment she moved. He was so in love with her, everything about her, her eyes, attitude, quirks and of course, her looks, he'd be a fool to discount their effect on him.

"It's a *Halloween* maze, honey." She took a step away and pulled him further down the small corridor. The moans and ghostly noises continued to cast their gloom overhead.

He rolled his eyes, letting her drag him along, barely hiding a smile. He let the sight of her round ass take his mind off where he was, instead sweeping him away to their bedroom just hours ago where more pleasurable moans and groans filled their tiny hotel room. He hoped the hotel walls were thick; otherwise, their neighbors already hated them probably.

Just wait until tonight. Hold on to that thought, Oscar, he told himself.

She slipped around the next corner, Oscar in tow, and stopped at a new fork in the corridor. She eyed the new path to her left, and then checked the one that continued in front of them.

"Keep going, or hang a left?" Florence asked.

"Whichever one gets us out of here," he begged.

"If I knew that, what would be the point of the maze, Oscar?" Florence asked, cocking her head and biting her lip.

"Right," he gave in. "You know I can't resist that."

She basked in her victory. He was incapable of denying her when she bit her lip and eyed him with her brow raised, his weakness.

"Let's go left," he decided with a light chuckle.

She yanked on his hand, retraining their path down the new corridor. The walls felt suffocating, painted in dark greys, reds and oranges. Splashes of what was meant to be blood peppered the wooden slats and the concrete. It appeared like some bloodbath with a paintbrush had happened in this very hall, or someone was using the maze as the canvas of some abstract art piece. Florence doubted the latter. Another ten feet down the hall, the two turned left with the bend in the maze and something jerked forward and howled.

The couple jumped back, reeling their arms back against the opposite wall. Florence was the first to laugh.

"That was good," she said, covering her up-turned mouth.

It was a bare skull atop a spike piercing clean through the top of the bone and down through the opening in the neck, its jaw bone sewn haphazardly shut with twine. The speaker hid behind the skull hurled another scream at them and the red glow intensified around it. They took a step to the right and the skull retreated back against the wall and the recording ceased, along with the red glow.

"Uh, honey?"

Florence felt Oscar's finger tapping her shoulder. She was focused on the skull. It was so cool.

"I know, right? That's so cool!" She glowed.

"Honey?" Oscar tried again, still tapping her shoulder.

"What, Oscar?" she said. "Look at how intricate this setup is."

"Honey!" Oscar raised his voice this time.

"Wha…" She stopped short as her eyes caught what Oscar was looking at. A figure stood at the opposite end. It, whoever it was, didn't move. Instead, it stared back at her, head tilted down. Electric green shone through the holes in the jack-o-lantern mask, obscuring most of its features in the darkened corridor. It wore a sports jacket and loosened tie, adorned in black slacks from the waist down. It was an odd clothing choice inside the maze. Then Florence saw the long sharp blade dangling in the figure's right hand.

"Hey!" Oscar yelled across the short distance, casting his voice over the wicked ambience. "We see you. Haha! You got us."

The figure didn't move. Its eyes appeared to stir with an evil intensity, emerald glowing vortexes behind a grisly pumpkin face.

"Okay, you got us," Florence repeated, not wanting to turn around and retreat, but not wanting to move forward toward the man, or woman, standing in their way. Of course it was an actor, but his aura was downright creepy.

A shrill scream broke through the music, but they didn't budge. Neither did it.

"Come on, man, let us…" Oscar stopped. Suddenly the figure's hand clenched tight around the knife and its arms began to swing, pumping in motion with thick strong legs, barreling forward.

"Just don't move, just don't move," Florence repeated. "It's another scare, it's not real."

Now it was at a full sprint, and Florence wished she had moved, that she would have turned and sprinted herself. Fear overrode her senses and she went to move just as the figure closed in.

"No!" Oscar screamed as a hand pushed him away, and the figure's knife-wielding hand swung forward and rammed into Florence's stomach.

Florence stumbled back by instinct. She felt nothing but the adrenaline pumping through her veins and a light tap on her stomach. She looked down, expecting to see blood and metal becoming one.

"Haha!" the man behind the mask bellowed, his voice deep and gruff under the grotesque mask. "I got ya!"

He pulled back the knife and a plastic blade slid back out of the handle as it left Florence's stomach. She knew it was stupid, but Florence reached down where the knife had landed and felt for a wound, still expecting to feel the icky moistness of blood. There was no hole, no blood. She sighed deeply and pulled in another breath.

"Are you serious?!" she yelled, momentarily overtaken by the fear that had seconds ago coursed through her veins. "You could give someone a fucking heart attack!"

"Oh, you're young," he told her, exchanging glances between her and Oscar. "Have fun. It only gets better from here."

Oscar grinned down at Florence, the edges of his lips peaking over his cheeks.

"He sure got you good!"

"Yeah, I know," she bit back, then softened her tone. "Guess that's what I get for dragging you in here."

Oscar smiled.

3

Kayden slipped around another corner, his mom and dad on his heels. The appearance and sudden disappearance of Pumpkinface, as Kayden had started calling him, had added an unexpected element to the maze. The website had not said a thing about live actors prowling the maze like some small version of SCarowinds. It *had* claimed to be "a family-friendly event for the whole family" though. Of course, the site looked like it hadn't been updated since the early 2000s, too. It didn't bother Kayden, but he would have appreciated a warning.

The shrill scream of a ghost pierced the silence and the music picked up with a beat that made Kayden lift his feet higher and walk a little quicker. The maze walls were much the same here, wooden planks, vines, red paint splattered haphazardly up their height and across the floor from time to time and the occasional pale red trail that looked like someone had drug a bleeding body across the concrete and forgot to clean up the evidence.

"I think we're going in circles," Tammy put a finger between her painted lips, absently chewing at a nail.

"Yeah," Kayden agreed, stopping a few feet before the next break in the corridor and turning to face his mom. He pointed behind himself toward one of the paths leading off down another direction. "I think we took the next right last time, though."

"Are you sure?" Tammy asked.

"Sort of..." Kayden admitted, raising his cheek and squinting his honey browns. "I mean, I think so. Isn't that the same owl up there?"

Kayden pointed a finger at a plastic owl with big yellow eyes, its head twitching from side to side like the gears inside were missing a few grooves. Tammy angled her head, examining the bird. Orange and red flashed in the distance and across the ceiling behind it, making it difficult to focus.

"I think he's right, Tammy," Ken finally spoke up. He'd remained mostly silent since the Pumpkinface incident.

Tammy nodded, shuffling her wavy brown locks over her shoulders.

"Well, let's go left instead then," she insisted.

She could barely see him to tell, but Kayden nodded in the dim light before swiveling around and leading them down the corridor. Past the hall that had led them back to this exact spot, Kayden turned to face the new piece of the maze. It was darker and a tighter fit. They couldn't walk side-by-side down it, maybe two at a time, but no more.

"Let's go," Kayden pushed and stepped into the corridor, squinting to see in the reduced light.

He thought his nose had adjusted to the rotten stench, but it was worse here, and kept getting worse the further he walked. Kayden covered his nose. Tammy and Ken did the same, grimacing.

"That's ripe," Ken blurted from under his shirt. "Where the hell do you get a smell like that for this?"

No one answered him. They kept walking. It continued to get darker, when suddenly a menacing red light shone down around them, illuminating something thick and meaty hanging on the wall.

Kayden stared into empty, clouded eyes as he stumbled back, clambering against the opposite wall.

"Calm down, Kayden," Tammy laughed. "It's just a dummy. A *really* realistic dummy."

"That's disgusting." Ken's fascination overrode the repulsion and smell. He stepped closer, examining the body.

It hung by a rope draped over the top of the wall, about a foot off the floor. The rope dug into the flesh of the dummy's neck. A massive open wound, painted in shades of black and blue, stretched from above the right ear, around the cheek and neck, and stopping just above the collarbone. The dummy's stained graphic t-shirt was in rags from the upper chest down, ribbons of cloth and fake flesh intermingling in a gruesome display of the macabre. The legs were missing altogether from the knees down.

"Definitely not 'family-friendly,' but look at the detail." Tammy shook her head.

"I found the leg, well, one of them," Kayden yelled, taking off at a slow jog toward where one of the dummy's severed legs laid. He reached down and picked up the limb. It was leathery, the skin pale like the body it belonged to. Kayden inspected the stump. He was amazed at the continued detail showing the bone, cut clean through, the meat and tendons forever stuck in place. He wanted to finger the mess of flesh and muscle out of some curious instinct, but he refrained.

"Put that down, Kayden," Tammy admonished him, more out of disgust than worry over getting in trouble. "You don't know who else has touched that."

Kayden shrugged and let the limb drop from his hands. It thumped against the concrete floor and came to a halt against the wall.

"This place is crazy cool," Kayden grinned, finally excited about the maze. His body was tense, every muscle and fiber ready, but the detail and effort put into the labyrinth was amazing, the real attempt at creating an atmosphere of fear. He could respect that. He reached into his pocket for his phone, he wanted to send a picture to Mira—she'd hate it, but he'd get a kick out of it—but his hand found an empty pocket.

Dammit, it's in that damn lockbox.

A scream howled through the darkness. Kayden tensed up but forced himself to relax.

"This place is crazy," Ken said, shaking his head emphatically. "*Crazy*, not cool."

4

"You think we're any closer to the end, Flo?" Oscar dared ask, knowing he probably sounded like a kid asking for the millionth time if they'd arrived yet.

"I think so. I mean, it's not like I know the layout, but I don't think we've got turned around again this time." Florence crept around another corner, ready just in case some ghost or spider might pop out around the corner. It didn't. "It can't be too much longer; it's not exactly the biggest maze. My family used to always do the corn mazes up in Peoria and we usually made it out within an hour. It was always a big thing back home."

She kept talking. It helped calm Oscar's nerves and she felt sort of bad for dragging him in here after assuring him it was just some pathetic little maze in some hick town. She had been wrong on the first count, and Oscar wasn't the scary movie type. He'd prefer a good thriller or sci-fi flick where the most blood you see is a gunshot wound or a skinned knee. Plus, Pumpkinface had genuinely scared the hell out of her earlier.

"There were a couple around town," she continued, walking next to Oscar as they came to the end of another corridor, eying their choices. "We always tried them all. I was pretty good at it usu…"

She stopped talking as they made the curve, letting the last syllable slip off her tongue after she caught her breath. "al."

It, he, was standing in the middle of the corridor. Pumpkinface.

Florence shook her head and grinned, looking over to her husband with an amused smile.

"Well, it looks like we meet again." She let her eyes go back to the stoic, mask-clad figure. His chest moved slowly, his oversized pumpkin head tilted to the right and then back to the left as if he was judging his prey. He held the same toy knife in his right hand. "We're not scared of you this time. You already got us earlier. Good job, by the way. You scared the shit out of me."

"Yeah," Oscar echoed her, winking as congratulations for addling his wife's nerves. "Good job, by the way, it takes a lot."

Florence squinted at her husband's attempt to sound big and bad.

"All right, well, we need to go that way." She pointed past Pumpkinface. "So, uh, we're just going to pass on by."

He didn't say a word, he didn't move, he just tilted his head from side to side. The electric green pulses of energy behind the massive eye sockets and blackened teeth sent chills down Florence's back. It was a creepy mask.

"Uh, okay," Florence stuttered again and pulled on Oscar's hand, motioning him to come on. She wasn't going to stand there in an eternal staring competition while the clock to get out in one hour was ticking away. By her watch they had passed the half hour mark and were quickly approaching the three-quarter hour mark.

They moved forward. Pumpkinface stood still, a stone atop concrete. Florence gulped, forcing herself not be so stupid. It was just someone dressed up trying to scare them, probably Jasper from out front, he was tall enough.

In the overcast shades of red and orange, the mask seemed to pulse, the deep beat of the creepy music keeping tune with Florence's heart. Pumpkinface wasn't moving, but she refused to act like a little girl.

Then his shoulders dropped and Pumpkinface bore down on the concrete and sprinted forward, arms swinging, knife glinting red and orange in the flashing lights. He closed the yard that separated them in less than a second, stabbing the knife forward into Oscar's stomach.

Oscar grunted, a look of terror glazing over his eyes.

"Oh, stop it!" Florence griped, slapping him on the shoulder as Pumpkinface enveloped Oscar in his big arms, pulling him close into a bear hug, holding the toy knife at his stomach. "I know it's fake, he got me earlier, you douchebag."

Goosebumps speckled her arms and she had to slow her breathing. It was fake, but everything combined scared the shit out of her in the second between Pumpkinface standing still, sprinting forward and acting like he was stabbing her husband.

"I…" Oscar tried.

"Oh, come on, Oscar, really?" Florence insisted. "I know it's fake, it's a damn Halloween maze. He got me, too, remember?"

Pumpkinface twisted his hand under Oscar's gut, shifting his head to look into Oscar's eyes. Oscar groaned and shuddered.

"Flo…" he tried. "R... Run!"

"What?" Florence took an involuntary step back, her brow crinkling, genuine worry starting to set in. "What?"

"Run!" Oscar screamed as Pumpkinface withdrew the knife. The solid metallic blade was drenched in warm, wet blood. Oscar's blood.

He kept his other arm grasped around Oscar but glanced down at the blade and then at Florence. It was like he wanted her to see what he'd done, like he was proud of it.

Florence backed up, her back colliding with the rough wooden wall.

"What the fuck?" she screamed, her mind spinning, tears held back by the confusion and panic.

"Run Fl—" Oscar tried, but a swift stab to the gut cut off his words and he bent forward in agony. The blade sunk into taut flesh and twisted. Pumpkinface wrenched the steel blade to the left, tearing open a wide tract of Oscar's flesh and stomach. Blood spilled between the rip in his white and blue polo.

With lightning speed, Pumpkinface retracted the blade and brought it about again, wedging it deep between Oscar's shoulder blade and collarbone. Oscar yelled as the knife twisted inside his shoulder, driving him to his knees.

The man withdrew the knife and turned to face Florence again. She was frozen in place, hands up, cupping her mouth in shock. She shook, tears already streaming down her cheeks.

"Run, Florence," Pumpkinface mimicked her husband who laid crumpled on the floor, his chest rising and falling in quick bursts. The man's voice was deep and menacing. "Make it a little challenging. Come on! Run, bitch!"

The wicked scream brought Florence back to reality and she spun to her left and raced down the open space. She didn't want to leave Oscar behind. She couldn't, but she kept running, something inside, beyond the now insignificant scares of the building and rushing music overhead, something wouldn't let her feet stop moving.

She hadn't made it a full ten steps before three quiet *pffts* echoed past her, followed by the searing pain of something long and hard piercing into her calf and the edge of her waist followed by the clang of metal against concrete. She went down hard, smashing her hands and face onto the concrete. The air rushed out of her lungs, and her side screamed as whatever was lodged in her skin hit the ground and twisted inside her body.

Florence screamed, the shriek piercing through the darkness and overwhelming the music with which it competed. Regaining some semblance of composure, she propped herself up on her side and dared a glance down at the wounded skin. Sticking out was the sharp point of a thick long nail, bloodied and dripping. About a foot south was the head of another nail embedded into the thick meat of her exposed calf, pushing the skin inward around the head.

"Well, that's love for you." The voice boomed over the music, a monotonous but gleeful cry from behind Pumpkinface's mask. He stood a few steps away from Oscar, tilting his head again like he was observing something interesting. "You think you know them. You marry them, and what do they do when someone stabs you in the *fucking* gut? They run like scared little bitches and leave you for the dogs."

Pain rushed up her side, nearly eclipsed by the anger that flared in Florence's chest. She wasn't a runner, she couldn't leave him. Placing her hands on the concrete, she pushed herself up, but the moment she let her weight fall on her injured leg, her body fell out from under her, sending her back to the cold concrete.

Pumpkinface stepped confidently forward, the nail gun casually slung over his shoulder in his right hand. Florence searched for the knife that had been in his hand, but she couldn't find it. She was about to move when a red glint caught her eye. Her gaze shot toward Oscar. His eyes met hers, scared and worried about her at the same moment. The knife was gouged through the palm of his left hand and stuck in the wall, pinning him in place with its blade along with a few long nails.

"Run, Flo!" he screamed weakly.

Florence gritted her teeth and tried to get to her feet again, but the pain was too much as the nail dug deeper into her calf, tearing away at the meat and tendon. She dropped to the floor again, but threw her arms out and began to drag herself forward.

"Well, I'm no dog, honey." Pumpkinface ignored Oscar's screams. Then his voice became quiet as his footsteps became quicker, reaching closer. He stood dangling his large eyes over her. Florence refused to look, but she knew he was there. He growled. "I'm the *fucking* devil."

A stout hand gripped around Florence's neck and lifted her off the floor. Her feet dangled in the air as her body was thrust against the wall, her face taking the brunt of the impact. Florence's eyes rolled back as her nose broke against the wooden plank, agony swept across her face as the blood began to pour from her nose and lip. She gasped for a breath to fill her empty lungs.

"No!" Oscar yelled. "Please don't! I'll do anything!"

The sound of the nail gun shooting another projectile didn't have time to assault Florence's ears before the nails began to shoot through her skin and pin her body to the wall. Pain jolted through her frame with each shot, starting at her left shoulder blade and running down her arm and then down her side and legs, until they finally worked their way back up to other shoulder blade.

Florence screamed with each piercing, as the skin and muscle was pulled taut against the wooden planks. Her body was suspended several inches off the ground, the nails holding her weight, tearing at her flesh and sinew beneath. She tried to scream again, but nothing would escape her lips. No noise could describe the pain. Her body shook as shock began to overtake her.

"Stop!" Oscar yelled again, trying to get Pumpkinface's attention. The man ignored him. "Why? Why are you doing this?"

Pumpkinface didn't bother to face Oscar, instead he stepped back and admired his art work, Florence tacked up against the wall, her skin splayed against the wood under each nail head. He admired the gentle curve of her neck, the way the nails pulled at her shoulders, the gaps between the nails and where they'd originally entered and the blood that seeped down her shirt. He let his eyes continue down, following the slope of her back, more nails, and then the curvature of her ass under those tiny shorts.

He stepped closer, hovering his right palm inches from Florence's buttocks, and looked to Oscar.

"The question is, why not?" He chortled quietly and moved to the side, putting Florence between himself and Oscar. "She really is beautiful, isn't she?"

"Get away from her, you freak!" Oscar moaned.

"Please, just let us go," Florence finally found the words, her voice minuscule and horrified. "Please."

"And ruin all the fun?" Pumpkinface mocked, clasping Florence's ass with his bare hand, earning a slight yelp from the woman. His head bobbed to the right, staring down at her body as he allowed his hand to drift further south. "No."

Florence sobbed, her body shaking uncontrollably. How was this happening? How had a simple trip to a maze turned into this? She shivered under the man's palm sliding against her backside, her eyes closed, but the tears still broke through the cracks.

His palm slid down her buttocks, but then he altered course and moved back up. He gripped tightly, moaning deeply under the mask before letting go.

"Too bad that's not part of the game," he lamented, letting his hand feel up her butt one more time. "Well, back to business."

"Just stop!" Oscar screamed, fear drenching his voice.

Florence tried to turn her head to see what Oscar saw, but it was no use. She felt it, though. The blade was cold against the inside of her right calf when it first touched. The first slice was almost more than she could take. She screamed, her voice breaking.

"Please. Please!" She begged as the blade slid back and forth, slicing into her leg. The serrated edge grabbed at her outer thigh and ripped a whole chunk of sinew and skin from her leg. It dangled from the knife, bobbing to and fro, blood dripping like rain pellets to the ground as the blade jerked back and forth. "Please stop, please!"

The blade ground to a halt when it met bone, jerking her whole body against the nails, scraping her against the wooden planks she was nailed to. Florence grunted, then sent up a prayer that it was over, begging God to stop this monster.

"Hmm…" Pumpkinface grunted. "I really need to get a bone saw."

Undeterred, he pulled the knife from the skin, earning a sickening suction from her wide-open thigh and a spit of crimson jumping into the growing pool below. Then he reared back and brought the knife back around with every ounce of strength in his thick body. It drove into her leg, past the torn flesh and wedged into the bone. He yanked it back again without wasting a single second and went back to work, cleaving skin and bone, ripping ribbons of flesh away from her leg with each blow. Blood and bits of muscle and tissue dislodged from the knife's blade and tumbled to the floor, coating it red. With one last chop, the blade went all the way through the bone, only stopping once it hit the muscle on the other side of the leg.

"Fuck!" Florence groaned as the pain overwhelmed her.

He began to saw again, the limb shaking and wobbling with each pull and shove of the blade, hanging only by a chord of muscle and skin. Finally, the muscle split in two and the skin snapped back, severed. Her right leg, from the knee down, dropped to the concrete irreverently. Blood poured like a spout from the stump under her calf and pooled around the severed limb.

"Now that you can't get away," Pumpkinface said, not an ounce of concern in his voice, "it's time to deal with the hubby. We can't let you have all the fun."

"I'm so sorry, honey," Oscar wept, reaching his free hand out to Florence. "I'm so sorry. I love you."

She couldn't form the words to say as the shock took over. It wasn't his fault, but the pain that coursed through her body was too overwhelming to utter a noise and the loss of blood was making her lightheaded. She watched as Pumpkinface trotted away toward Oscar. He turned and looked at Florence once he was in place, like he wanted to be sure she was watching.

He sheathed the spare knife and pulled the nail gun back over his shoulder and got his grip right on the handle before angling it down at Oscar. The first shot pierced the top of Oscar's foot. He shrieked, but the music was overbearing, masking his plea. The next two stuck into his knee and lower thigh.

"You sick fuck!" Oscar bellowed. "What do you want?"

The answer came as a nail to the groin. Oscar screamed.

Pumpkinface maneuvered the business end of the nail gun up and lined it up with palm of Oscar's hand. He pulled the trigger and sent a volley of new nails into Oscar's hand, and for good measure a few down his wrist and arm, pinning him tightly to the wall.

Oscar's screams broke Florence's heart even as the lack of blood began to sap away her energy. Her vision began to blur, but she quickly blinked away the haze.

The nail gun dropped to the floor with a heavy clatter and Pumpkinface grasped the knife in Oscar's hand and reeled back, splaying open Oscar's palm as the blade tore away from the wall. Blood poured over Oscar's palm, over the ripped layers of skin that dangled flaccid toward the ground. Then the man crouched down and slammed the knife into the existing wound in Oscar's stomach, but this time he cleaved open a gap up to Oscar's ribcage. The blade stopped abruptly when it caught against the bone, jerking Oscar's body off the ground at the impact and earning a grunt from the newlywed.

Pumpkinface drew back on the knife, freeing the blade from his victim's body and sending droplets of blood careening across the concrete and the opposite wall. Florence couldn't see the man's smile, but she could imagine it. In all the man's abject need for pain, she could visualize a wicked grin across his lips. She hated him, wanted him dead.

He growled. It was a guttural, almost animalistic noise, before he drove his hands into the gap his knife had carved in Oscar's chest. His fingers laced beneath the skin, fat, and sinew, gripping tightly, and tugged back. Skin peeled outward and muscle tore under his grasp. The blood gurgled up through Oscar's open stomach and chest, his organs visible to anyone who might wander by.

"Plea… St… Stop," Oscar tried as the man let go and then dove his hands back inside, enveloping a section of Oscar's small intestine in his warm hands. They were slick and slimy, coated in blood and gelatinous material that gave way to the man's strong hands. He reeled back, pulling the intestine away from Oscar's body and out into the world. He kept pulling, wrapping a section of the meaty chord around his hand.

"Ug…" Oscar moaned and wretched, his body convulsing at the pain and sensation of his insides being torn from his body.

Pumpkinface stood erect again. He sighed before stepping forward and walking back across the corridor in Florence's direction. Oscar's intestines remained in hand, still stringing out from the man's stomach, thick drops of blood dripping across the concrete. He stopped beside Florence and looked around her for a moment before settling on his objective. He jerked hard on the slippery meat in his hands, pulling out another few feet. The chord of muscle slapped against the floor. Then he reeled in the slack and threw the end of Oscar's small intestine around Florence's neck, stapling the end right next to her face.

"Stop," Florence begged between stuttered breaths, finally managing to take control of her voice again.

"But I'm not done," he told her just before he sunk the knife into her side and pulled up hard, splitting her side open. "I have to join you two together."

He said it like there was no alternative, as if it was a moral imperative that he completes his task. Despite the pain, Florence angled her head away from the wall and squinted at the man, confused and disgusted.

As her vision began to darken, she felt something large and foreign invade her side where the knife had cleaved her open. She screamed as pain bloomed from the presence of Pumpkinface's hands expanding in her side, grasping for something, fingers stretching and contracting between her guts. The feeling rushed into her brain and nearly overloaded her senses. Then the pain changed as he pulled out his hand, tugging her insides out through the hole he'd created. She dared to glance down as he lifted something round and bloody up to meet her baby blue eyes. It was her own small intestine. She considered it, eyes drawn tight, her lips trembling.

"Almost done," he said, like it was nothing big, only a job to be completed.

He stepped away and her body seized up as her longest organ began to tighten inside her and then wiggled through her side and out into the open air. Her body convulsed under the unnatural sensation of her insides exiting her flesh. She caught glimpses through dimmed eyes as he pulled her intestines away and stood next to Oscar. She couldn't look that far down, but she knew that if she could, she'd see the other end of the long mass that Pumpkinface had strewn from her depths to where he now stood.

"Ah, dammit. He's already dead." Pumpkinface shrugged, like it was no worse than a dead ant or roach.

"No!" Florence screamed, ignoring the pain in her side. She struggled, trying to get loose, but the pain was overwhelming and the nails only ripped at her skin. Her body was wracked in pain and emotional agony. He was gone. "No!"

Pumpkinface retrieved the nail gun again from his shoulder, ignoring her screams. He yanked another couple feet of intestine from Florence's body, earning a deep groan and a splattering of blood on the concrete, and placed the other end against Oscar's temple.

"'Til death do you part," Pumpkinface mocked and shoved the edge of the nail gun against Oscar's head and pulled the trigger, pinning Florence's intestine to Oscar's forehead and sending a nail straight into Oscar's brain. Oscar's head jerked back with a splatter of red.

Pumpkinface chortled deeply as Florence screamed, and almost pranced over to her. He shoved the squishy wet end of Oscar's intestine against her forehead. "Now it's your turn, darling. 'Til death do you part."

The last thing she saw was the tip of the nail gun followed by the tiny sound of rushing air.

5

"Are we turned around again?" Ken frowned cynically. "I swear I've seen this spot before."

"I don't think so, hon," Tammy tried to console him.

Ken was beginning to feel claustrophobic, trapped. Each time they found themselves headed down another familiar hall, the more Ken fretted. This one was a familiar hall, the one they had started at in fact, but Tammy felt it best to withhold that tidbit of information, for her husband's benefit.

"Yeah, we are," Kayden disagreed. He couldn't see his mother's pursed lips and glare, trying to tell him to shut up in the dark red glow of the hall. "This is *literally* where we started."

"Are you serious?" Ken almost shouted. His voice carried over the music and well past Kayden's ears. Kayden winced, finally realizing what his mom had been trying to communicate.

Sorry, he mouthed.

Tammy rolled her eyes and put a consoling hand on Ken's shoulder, pressing him forward, down a different hall than they had originally chosen.

"We'll just try this path this time. Maybe we'll have better luck," she tried. "Just calm down, hon."

Ken gulped in a deep breath and Kayden followed along for a moment before whipping around them to take the lead. His dad might not like it, but Kayden thought it was great. The creepy music, the old cheap animatronics, precisely placed motion detectors ready to spring some scare around the corner. That's not to say that it didn't make his heart race when some skeleton came popping out of the shadows a corridor or two back, though.

"Don't wander off now, Kayden. We don't need to get split up." Tammy admonished the boy, waving with her free hand for him to come back.

He slowed his trot but kept a few feet ahead. He scanned the room, considering each wooden slat that formed a set of parallel walls, the corners where they met the cold concrete below, the dark rafters that hung above him. Kayden had caught on to the setup. At various locations, motion cameras had been cut into small holes in the wood to catch the maze walkers. Setting one off always sprung some well-placed scare just in time for the passerby to garner the full effect. So far, nothing.

They turned down another hall, splitting off to the left after Ken and Tammy argued for a good two minutes over which direction made the most sense, as if either of them had a clue which was really right. Kayden leaned back against the wall, eyebrow raised, watching. Finally, they took the left. Less than halfway down the new corridor, Kayden stopped them and pointed to an indention in the wall.

"Look," he directed them, showing them the location of one of motion cameras. "There must be another trap up here."

His parents were silent as they followed close behind Kayden. He stalked carefully forward, examining the walls and floor nearby. Apart from the natural imperfections in the wood, red paint splatters and the occasional fake strand of vine and spider web, the walls were unscathed. No telltale lines, other marks or indentations.

Kayden huffed, confused. *Might as well test it.*

He stepped forward, through the camera's field of view. At first there was nothing, then a whooshing noise rushed in from overhead. He craned his neck back as a massive spider, with at least a two-foot leg span, careened down over their heads only to stop a foot above them. He jerked, closing his eyes and sighing. He hated spiders.

Dammit, he exclaimed inside his head, pulling his eyes away from the spider and finding his parents grinning at him.

"Just a spider," Tammy said.

"I know," Kayden almost bit back, but he caught himself just in time and softened his tone.

"All right, let's move on," Ken instructed and passed under the dangling arthropod. He slipped by Kayden as the boy turned around, and passed him on down the hallway, making the next turn. "Let's get..."

Kayden cocked his head to the side, watching the horrified expression on his dad's frozen face. He exchanged glances with his mom, and they quickened their steps.

"No! Stay back," Ken tried, but it was too late.

Tammy screamed when she made the corner, a shrill piercing noise, louder than any that had yet broken through the music. Everything in his parents' reaction to what lie around the corner told Kayden to stay rooted where he was, but curiosity drove him to move. Confused and worried, Kayden stepped past the bend and his eyes immediately met the source of his parents' horror.

It was the newlywed couple. Tammy dropped behind Kayden and covered his eyes, but he brushed her hand away. His eyes had already taken in enough to know what horrified them. He knew that even if he was blinded for life, the sight would still be seared into his mind.

The first thing his eye caught was the severed leg. It laid carelessly on the concrete, bisected just above the knee, a rag of tattered flesh at the stump, lying in a pool of the girl's blood. Then his eyes found the girl, her body nailed like some sign against the wall, her remaining leg dangling inches above the ground. Blood still fell from the stump under her thigh, the cut fresh.

Kayden stumbled back, letting his weight fall against his mom. His mind was blaring. *The leg I picked up earlier…was that real?* A new shiver strung up his body. He gulped, a sense of nausea slipping into his stomach.

The skin around the edge of her leg, her waist and arms were stretched out, tugging against the nails that held her body to the wall, blood dribbling over every spare inch of her skin. Her head was angled away from Kayden, but he could see something long and slimy connected to her face.

In the brief second before his mom had tried to shield his eyes, his gaze had streaked like lightning across the long string and landed with a gasp when he realized where it ended. Inside Oscar's wide-open stomach. Intestines, Oscar's intestines.

The man's hand was nailed flat against the wall next to where his body sprawled back limply on the concrete, more nails protruding from his feet and leg. His head was held up by another string of intestines affixed nauseatingly to his temple. Kayden followed the small organ back to Florence's side.

Tammy released her grip around Kayden, bent over and wretched onto the floor. Kayden felt like doing the same, but swallowed, refusing to let himself lose his lunch.

"What type of sicko does something like this?" Ken gasped, stepping backward. He lifted his shirt at the waist and withdrew a small compact pistol, the 9mm Springfield Kayden knew he always carried, ignoring the *No Weapons Allowed* signs whenever they popped up. "We've got to get out of here, now!"

He about-faced, holding the pistol low but ready, and pushed Tammy and Kayden back the direction they'd come. "Let's get back to the entry. Now!"

Kayden went to run, but remembered what the shopkeeper had said when he led them into the maze.

"The man at the desk said the door would be locked," Kayden reminded them as he stumbled for a moment before regaining his footing, his words running into each other as they spewed out in fear.

"Maybe it's just a ruse," Tammy hoped. "Maybe it's just meant to keep us in the maze."

"Listen to your mom," Ken commanded as they took off, spreading their legs to their max. It wasn't meant to be condescending or domineering, it was only meant to get them moving.

The red and orange lights began to strobe. Kayden squinted, noting the sudden change in their pattern which strained his vision, trying to adjust to the frantic flashing. He shot forward, images of the severed leg and string of intestines flashing into his mind with the incessant rhythm of the strobing lights. His mind replayed him picking up the severed leg of the earlier cadaver over and over.

It was *real! This can't be happening.*

A skeleton pounced out of the wall to their right as they triggered the motion sensor. Adrenaline pumping, Kayden nearly lost his balance, swerving into his mom and tumbling against the wall before planting his feet firmly beneath himself again. His feet pounded the concrete, breath panting, his parents hot on his trail.

Kayden careened around the last corner and fixed the entry

door in his sights. Oscar's cold dead gaze flashed in his mind and Kayden jerked to the side before realizing it was all in his head. The lights flashed. Kayden continued to pump his lean legs, the gap between him and his parents widening.

He thrust past the last fork in the maze, end in sight, when a grunt and clatter behind him stole his attention. Something metal clanged against the floor. His dad yelled, and his mom screamed. Kayden ground to a halt and spun on his feet.

"Dad!" Kayden squelched, honey brown eyes wide in terror at the sight of blood flowing down his dad's chest.

Pumpkinface was getting back to his feet, hovering over Kenneth's body. He yanked the serrated blade out of Ken's chest, tearing away a chunk of fat and muscle. Strings of something meaty, matted in crimson and shades of blue and purple, dangled from the knife. Ken's eyes fluttered and he groaned.

"No!" Tammy yelled, throwing herself on the masked man.

"No!" Kayden echoed, but it was too late. Kayden witnessed the tip of the same blade burst through his mom's back just above her pelvic bone. "No!"

"Ru...run, Kayden! Run!" Ken screamed, before fixing his eyes on the freak in the mask as the blade was ripped from Tammy's stomach. She fell against the wall, hands clutching her body.

"No. I..." Kayden tried. He couldn't leave them here, not like this.

"Run!" Ken bellowed, blood gurgling between his lips.

Kayden stepped toward them, wanting to do something, anything.

The towering figure returned his attention to Ken, intent on finishing what he'd started. He reared the slender metallic edge back and slashed forward. The blade melted through the thin skin and muscle holding his mouth together. His jaw flopped down, a heavy piece of flesh and bone, dangling without purpose. A sanguine river burst from his mouth, pouring down his neck, obscuring the grotesque mass.

Kayden stared wide-eyed at his dad, eyes trapped by the jaw hanging useless by a slender strand of muscle at the back of his mouth, a gaping void where his lower jaw should have been. He went to move, but it was too late. His dad's chest had stopped rising and his eyes were no longer filled with fear, his empty gunmetal grey eyes peered upward without purpose. Kayden tried to scream but his mouth wouldn't move as emotions flooded his heart.

"N-" his mother began, but her scream was cut short by the piercing edge of the blade as it slid through her throat like butter. Blood seeped around the entry and exit of the blade.

"Run, boy!" the man behind the mask growled.

Something in the voice crept deep beneath Kayden's skin. He faltered back a step, but stopped, his body frozen in place, mortified by the image before him.

"Mom!" he finally managed to scream.

In response, Pumpkinface twisted the blade, slicing down further into Tammy's neck and then wrenched the knife to the left, ripping it out, cleaving her neck in half. Her head flopped aimlessly to her shoulder, blood spouting from the gaping hole. Blood splattered across Pumpkinface's mask and dripped to the floor.

Kayden stopped, mortified, tears trailing down his cheeks. Then Pumpkinface's gaze flicked toward Kayden, his empty green glowing sockets falling menacingly on the boy.

"I said run, boy!" he repeated.

Kayden didn't move, less an act of stubborn horrified rebellion than the sudden paralysis that had overcome him. He couldn't say why he remained. He needed to run, he wanted to run, but the gruesome sight of his parents in pools of blood on the ground shook him to his very core, momentarily squelching his ability to reason or move.

"Run!" The guttural scream shook Kayden at his core as Pumpkinface shoved Tammy's body to the ground with an irreverent thud.

Shaken from his stupor, Kayden spun around and sprinted for the entry door. In a few long strides, he was there. He spun the handle, but it jerked against his hand. Locked.

Dammit! He wasn't lying.

He turned and eyed the masked man, his back turned to Kayden, busy doing something out of sight. There were two other routes, but the past fifty minutes had made one thing abundantly clear. He didn't know how to get out, except for the door at his back where they had all entered, and it was locked. His eyes jerked between the two alternative paths. He had no real choice, so he chose the far-right path at random.

Kayden shoved off the concrete and barreled down his chosen path, careening around each corner. He didn't know where he was headed. The path was new to him after the third bend, its corridors bathed in strobing orange and red. The splotches and smears of blood were frightening to his eyes now, real and horrifying. He refused to imagine how they had found their way there, instead focusing the pumping of legs, letting all that running up and down the basketball court finally be put to good use.

He skidded to a stop at a dead-end, leaning over with his hands propped against his knees. His cheeks ballooned as he forced the air from his lungs and took another drag of rotten air, closing his eyes just long enough to catch his breath. Turning, he bolted off again, and took the left at the intersecting corridors. Kayden refused to slow around the next corner. His arm beat against the wooden wall, nearly knocking him off balance, but he made it, one step further away from the freak.

Was Pumpkinface behind him? Was he even following?

Kayden slowed to a jog and dared a look to his rear. Nothing. *Where is he?*

He returned his attention forward and accelerated to a run, slowing just enough to make the next bend in the maze, before sprinting at full speed again. It didn't matter if the man was behind him, he had to get out. He hadn't seen this part of the maze before. It was all new, more unknown, but with it the hope of an exit.

Screams echoed from the loud speakers again. His body convulsed in fear before he realized what it was, his legs clenching, sending his body tumbling to the ground. Arms outstretched, his palms took the brunt of the impact, lightening the fall against his hip and chest. His chin clapped against the concrete. Lightning coursed up his face. Kayden squinted, trying to bear the pain.

"Agh!" he groaned. He reached up and cupped his chin, just as the taste of iron found his tongue, blood. He pulled his hand back at the feeling of the liquid on his chin.

Kayden gritted his teeth, not wasting a second before he shook off the pain and got back to his feet. As his vision cleared, he was amazed at what he found just ten yards ahead. A door. His eyes gleamed.

The exit.

A smile upended the scowl on Kayden's face as his legs started to carry him forward. He crossed past an intersection in the maze, only yards away from his salvation. He could feel the cool air seeping through cracks in the doorframe and see the slender beams of light breaking into the darkness.

Suddenly a sharp pain pierced through the thick meat of his hip, pushing him off kilter. His left leg went limp for a brief second, but it was just enough to take him to the ground again. He collapsed to the floor, sprawled out on his side. He gripped his hip, fingers touching a small metallic circle just below his waist. Kayden squirmed to get back to his feet, but the feeling of something long and steely puncturing his insides brought him back to the floor. He screamed.

A shuffling to his left stole his attention and he bolted his eyes toward the dark intersection he had just passed. Out of the darkness stepped Pumpkinface, the nail gun in hand. He raised his other hand, a pistol in his grasp. His dad's pistol.

Kayden gulped and began to squirm away on his rear. He needed to get away. The exit was so close.

"Your dad tried to kill me with this," Pumpkinface growled, shifting his head from side to side as he stepped closer and closer to Kayden. He sprinted the feet between them, planting a foot on Kayden's calf and bearing down. Kayden grimaced, trying to yank his leg loose.

"Get off me!"

Pumpkinface laughed under his mask.

"Maybe you can do better. At least this'll make it a little more sportsman-like of me," the masked man said. He extended his gun-wielding hand and abruptly tossed the weapon off toward the door. It clattered to the concrete, sliding to a stop only a few feet past Kayden, a mere two yards from the exit. "It's not like you'll actually get it. Oh, and I cut your mom's head off. I was going to bring it to show you, but I can only carry so much."

With Kayden's eyes on the gun and the anger spouting up his spine, the man made his move, leaping and bringing his body down on top of Kayden. The knife swung through the air. Catching the sudden movement at the edge of his vision, Kayden flung his face around just in time to see the blade stab into his shoulder.

He screamed, instinctively raising his hands and pushing back against the man, one hand sprawled against the pumpkin face. His fingers searched for any vulnerability, but the mask was sealed tight. The eerie green glow shone from the mask, basking Kayden in a swirl of green.

Pumpkinface rose from his crouch, freeing his face from the boy's grasp, and bore his eyes down on Kayden. He tilted his head to the right and then back to the left as he planted his full weight on Kayden's body, pinning him to the ground. Kayden let his mouth hang open as he gasped, fear flooding every part of his being as the pain rushed up his shoulder. He struggled to escape Pumpkinface's iron grip.

"You're not going anywhere, boy!" he rumbled into Kayden's face.

Kayden thrashed, trying to knock the man off balance, but it was useless. The more the knife dug into his shoulder, the more pain jolted up his side, and the less movement he managed to get from the limb. As his resolve began to break down, a thought hit Kayden. It would hurt like hell, but it might just give him a chance. He had to try.

Kayden let his left hand let go of the man, as the knife continued to wedge between bone and skin. Free, he reached down to his hip and found the metallic head of the nail embedded in his side. Keeping his eyes bound to Pumpkinface's green glows, he gripped the nail head between his fingers and clenched his teeth.

He took in a deep breath and yanked as hard and quickly as he could manage.

Pumpkinface jerked to the side, not sure what had just happened. Then Kayden swung the nail up and jabbed it into the freak's neck. Pumpkinface jerked his hand back, reeling the knife out of Kayden's shoulder. His hands rushed to the nail in his neck, flipping his body of off Kayden. Kayden flipped over and jumped to his feet.

A streak of pain jumped up his right leg and his body flailed back to the ground. He caught himself in time to keep his face from smacking against the concrete. Groaning, he twisted just enough to check his leg where the pain had come from. His eyes found the deep cut under his calf, it was at least half-an-inch deep, sanguine liquid coating the leg below it and dripping on the floor. He reached down to touch it instinctively, but he reeled back as the touch sent another agonizing pulse up his side. In the corner of his vision he saw Pumpkinface staring at him, holding his neck, assessing him.

"Go away!" Kayden yelled aimlessly between sobs. "Leave me alone!"

He ignored the boy. Instead, body on the ground, he raised the nail gun in his left hand and pointed it at Kayden.

"Now it's your turn, you fucking little bitch," growled Pumpkinface as he jerked forward, daring to let go of his neck long enough to get to his feet. Blood flooded down his neck.

On his ass, Kayden drug himself backward as quick as could manage, attempting to lift his body off the ground with his hands and one good leg, trying not to disturb the new wound. Red and orange flashed across his vision. He inched back as Pumpkinface stole a foot to his every inch.

"Go away!" Kayden tried again. "Go to hell, you freak!"

There was no emotion on the pumpkin mask as the man's feet landed a step away from Kayden and then his other foot stomped down onto Kayden's injured leg, slamming the open cut against the concrete.

Kayden shrieked as the foot grinded his calf from side to side on the rough concrete, opening and stretching the wound, grating the fresh muscle against the dirty floor. Blood smeared across the floor and Kayden moaned with each movement of the man's foot.

"Look at me!" Pumpkinface growled, the words more difficult to speak that just minutes ago, but Kayden refused. "*Fucking* look at me!"

When Kayden didn't listen, he lifted his foot and brought it back down, causing the cut to widen as it smashed against the ground again. Then he threw the nail gun over his shoulder and reached his fingers up to the neck of his mask and lifted, his other hand still grasping the nail in his neck. Kayden's eyes shot to the man, curiosity baiting his attention. The mask lifted. Kayden gasped. Why had he not guessed?

It was Jasper; his empty green eyes stared back at Kayden as he tossed the pumpkin mask to the floor. His broad shoulders seemed less menacing now, but Kayden knew who he was, what he was. A monster in the maze.

"You should be proud," Jasper told him. "You're going to be the last to die. Unfortunately, that means it's going to be the most painful, but you lasted the longest. I think I'll display your body right at the entrance."

"You sick freak!" Kayden blurted. He tried to squirm out from under Jasper, but as soon as he slipped free he knew it would only be a momentary reprieve.

"Do you want to know why?" Jasper asked, a stoic smile over his lips.

Kayden didn't answer. It didn't matter, knowing wouldn't change anything. His lips trembled as his entire body shook, wracked with pain, fear and grief.

"It's simple," Jasper told him, the edges of his lips rising under his green eyes. "Because I can."

The man was crazy, his mind lost to some demented world.

Kayden flipped onto his stomach and began to crawl on all fours, trying to focus on the need to escape, adrenaline blocking the pain coming from his leg. He slapped his palms onto the concrete and pulled himself forward, using his uninjured leg to push his body forward. He imagined the trail of blood that he'd be leaving, the trail that some unsuspecting person would soon think was just a trail of paint made to look like blood, unless he escaped.

Suddenly, something cold and metallic stabbed into Kayden's side, glancing his waist, barely missing a fatal blow to his midsection. Kayden flinched to the right as Jasper had to rebound to hold his neck. He drug himself forward a few more feet, as calm footsteps followed along. Jasper was in no hurry, and it occurred to Kayden that there was nothing he could do.

I'm going to die here.

A new tear broke down his cheek. *Why? Why is this happening?* But there was no answer. It was simple, random, evil. A mad man who got his kicks off some bloody fetish.

In the edge of his sight, Kayden caught Jasper's feet as they stopped. He went to turn, to see why Jasper had stopped. The man knelt down to his knees and before Kayden could see what he was doing, the cold steel of the knife pierced into his left arm just below his shoulder, into the same wound the man had created just moments ago.

Kayden wailed. "Please stop, just let me go."

"Let you go?" Jasper questioned, his voice deep, but nothing like it had been within the mask. "Do you think I'm stupid?"

"I promise, I won't say a thing," Kayden begged, hoping that something in this man's mental state would make him susceptible to his lies.

"You *do* think I'm stupid, don't you?" Jasper asked. "Even if you wouldn't say anything, I'd prefer to keep you here. I like my trophies."

Before Kayden could utter another word, Jasper dug the knife deeper into Kayden's arm, severing a tendon in his shoulder and forcing the knife out the other side. Kayden screamed as the blood spat from his arm. Jasper was not deterred.

He reeled back on the knife, ripping the thin layer of skin on Kayden's upper arm from his body and tearing the tightened bicep from its place. Blood poured from his shoulder, pooling on the ground, as the meat gripped to the blade. As the blade came back down and met with hard bone, Jasper began to hack at the dense matter. Kayden felt it begin to crack under the immense pressure of each blow. He tried to move but he couldn't.

"Please!" Kayden cried. It was useless, but he had to say something. The pain was too intense, bursting up his shoulder and exploding in his brain.

Finally the bone broke, and only the muscle under his arm kept the limb attached. Jasper got back to his feet, then reached down and gripped his fingers around the wrist of Kayden's partially severed arm, planting his foot on Kayden's chest.

"What are you doing?" Kayden pleaded.

Jasper grinned wickedly and succinctly, "I'm taking your

arm."

"Wh—" Kayden's question was cut off by a pain unlike anything he'd ever felt as Jasper wrenched at his arm, tugging against the remaining muscle and flesh that tethered it to Kayden's body.

"Stop! Please!" Kayden screamed between each throb of pain up his arm and spine, placing every ounce of being he had left inside into his pleas.

"Shut up, you little pussy!" Jasper yelled back, annoyed.

He jerked Kayden's arm again, twisting it back and forth. The meat and flesh screamed in agony as the muscle began to rip. Kayden clenched his teeth and looked away, fixing his eyes away from Jasper and his arm. Pain blossomed in Kayden's head as the last fiber and sinew snapped and his arm ripped from his body. His eyes shot open in pain.

He didn't think in that moment that he'd ever feel hope again, but there it was, staring right back at him. The barrel of his dad's 9mm, and a sudden sense of euphoria, a detachment from all that was happening around him. A sudden rush of hope flushed through his body and Kayden slung out his remaining arm, wrapping his fingers around the barrel. He didn't care if Jasper saw him, he just needed one chance. He spun the gun around and grasped the small stock of the compact weapon.

"What are…" Jasper sounded confused, Kayden's severed arm dangling in his grasp. Kayden didn't even notice the limb, or the grisly tattered flesh where countless crimson beads fell and splattered his chest.

Kayden threw himself onto his back, feeling the pain surge through his body as the stub of his shoulder ground against concrete. He drew on everything his dad had taught him at the range in Charlotte from the time he was in elementary school. It all streamed through his mind in less than a second.

Finger off the trigger until you're ready to fire. Don't look at the crosshairs, look past them, at the target.

He found Jasper in his sights, his sea green eyes awestruck.

Release the safety.

Kayden flipped the safety lever and put his finger on the trigger.

Fire away.

He pulled the trigger. The boom was deafening in the enclosed space and for a second the flash at the end of the barrel challenged the strobe lights for dominance. Kayden saw the bullet find its home in Jasper's chest, just below his neck, as a splat of blood soaked his chest and ejected out of Jasper's back. Kayden pulled the trigger again, and again. Bullets flew, riddling Jasper's body. He jerked violently, his eyes wide and scared. He lugged backward, teetering to the right and then the left, his eyes fluttering in bewilderment.

"How?" Jasper stuttered as blood slurped out of his mouth. "You?"

The man's green eyes went blank and his body slumped to the ground with a thud.

Kayden let his hand drop, slapping the metal casing of the pistol on the ground. The lights continued to flash, but there was no more movement. Kayden took in a deep breath and tried to steady his nerves. His whole body shook, shivering as the adrenaline worked its way through his veins. Finally, he loosened his grip on the pistol, but refused to let it go. He shuddered under the pain.

I'm alive.

He pushed himself up on his good elbow, working to ignore the pain, grunting as each movement sent another jolt through his spine.

I've got to get out of here.

Kayden looked around him, at all the mayhem. The flashing lights, the blood-splattered wood, Jasper's dead body, the thought of his mom and dad's lifeless forms somewhere deep in the maze. He wanted to find them, to stay there with them forever, but he knew he had to get out, he had to survive.

"I love you, Mom," he said into the flashing lights. "I love you, Dad. I'm so sorry."

As he broke down in tears, Kayden reluctantly slid his body across the concrete, his blood painting the floor, ragged flesh scraping the ground. At the exit, he reached up and tried the handle. Locked.

"Dammit!" he muttered.

He eyed the gun in his hand, and his eyebrows rose. He looked at the door handle, aimed the pistol at it and fired. Metal and wood splintered and burst as the door swung open, bathing Kayden's face in cool air and gentle rays of sunlight.

He squinted, adjusting his eyes to the outside glare. A car flew by on the small country road just ten yards around the corner.

I've got to get to the road.

Kayden reached up with his remaining arm and gripped the splintered door frame. He pressed his body against the frame and struggled to drag himself to his feet. He let his eyes stray to the bloody stump where his left arm had once hung. He swore he could feel the limb even though his eyes confirmed it was gone, nothing more than tattered strings of muscle and flesh. His body shook.

He stumbled forward, almost crashing to the gravel when his right foot found purchase on the ground, sending an intolerable jolt of pain up his side from the wound in his hip. Instead, Kayden slapped against the wooden frame of the warehouse, the bloody stump scraping against rough boards as he tried to keep his foot up. He looked down. Blood flowed from the gaping slice on his leg and stump by his shoulder.

Move, Kayden!

Kayden screamed, willing himself forward. He forced his foot down, bearing the pain that shot up his side and yelling a string of curses as a blood trail formed along the wall. He slid forward, but stopped at the corner. His head spun at the massive loss of blood. He struggled to steady himself, fixing his weak gaze on the road a few yards away.

Trying to ignore the pain, he shook his head and balanced himself. He found the Taurus out front along with the truck and other sedan. They were of no use to him, he didn't have the keys and didn't have a clue how to hotwire a car. He fixed his eyes on the road again and steeled himself against the pain as the roar of an engine in the distance found his ears. He took in a deep breath and pushed himself around the corner, leaving the support of the wall. Kayden barreled forward, gravel crunching under his feet.

But the pain was too much. Before he could make it three steps, his leg couldn't take anymore and his body collapsed, slamming hard against the gravel into a roll. His body twisted and bounced along the rock-filled parking lot.

"Fuck!" he groaned when his body finally came to a stop only three feet from the paved blacktop.

The whir of the car's engine was getting closer by the second. Kayden grunted, digging his fingers into the gravel and drug himself toward the road. Only another foot. He used his good leg to push his body another few inches. The sound grew louder as a burnt orange Camaro careened around the corner from behind a hedge of nearly leafless trees, its engine blaring.

"Stop!" Kayden screamed, his voice weak and quiet. He shoved forward one more time, throwing his body onto the black-top, into the path of the car. He waved his remaining arm in the air, frantically waving down the driver.

Tires screeched as the car neared, fishtailing to a halt barely a full car-length from Kayden's torn body. The door clicked open and feet thudded against the pavement.

I'm going to make it.

ABOUT THE AUTHOR

Jordon Greene is the Award-Winning & Amazon Bestselling Horror Author of *To Watch You Bleed* and *They'll Call It Treason*. He is a full stack web developer for the nation's largest privately owned shoe retailer and a graduate of UNC Charlotte. Jordon spends his time building web applications, attempting to sing along to his favorite rock songs, driving way too fast, and reading. He lives in Concord, NC just close enough and just far enough away from Charlotte.

Visit Jordon Online

www.JordonGreene.com

If you enjoyed this story,
please consider reviewing it online at retailers like Amazon
and recommending it to friends and family.